June 2001

Sam —

Have fun on your
first trip to
Martha's Vineyard!

Love,

MAX Gama Betsey

Barnaby's Kite Ride

Written and Illustrated
by Wendy W. Rouillard

For ordering information, write or telephone:

BARNABY & COMPANY PUBLISHING AND PRODUCTIONS, L.L.C.

P.O. Box 3198
Nantucket, MA 02584
tel: 508-228-5114
888-5-BARNABY
Email: barnaby@nantucket.net

ISBN 0-9642836-6-2
Library of Congress Catalog Card Number: 98-92482

Summary: Stuck inside the house on a cold, snowy winter day, Barnaby and Baxter imagine themselves on a summer kite ride adventure.

BARNABY BOOK #4
Second Edition

Visit Barnaby's Web Site!
www.barnabybear.com

Barnaby's Kite Ride

On a snowy day in January, Barnaby and Baxter sat inside, longing for the days of summer.

"I wish we could go outside to fly our kite," said Baxter.

Barnaby gazed at the photograph of them on the wall, remembering the time they had visited the Island of Martha's Vineyard.

"What fun it was, flying our kite," said Barnaby with a sigh.

He wiped the frost from the window and watched the giant snowflakes falling from the sky. His mind began to drift back to those warm summer days…

DAYDREAMING
IN
WINTER

Suddenly, Barnaby imagined that he and Baxter were flying their kite at the Edgartown Lighthouse. In his mind it was no longer a cold winter day, but a sunny summer day on Martha's Vineyard.

"What a perfect day to fly our kite," said Barnaby cheerfully. "The wind is just right."

But all of a sudden, there was a gust of wind. It was so strong that the kite began to drag Barnaby across the sand!

Baxter tried to help. He grabbed Barnaby. But the kite pulled them up, up, into the air.

"OH BOY!" shouted Barnaby.

"OH NO!" cried Baxter.

Off they went, flying high in the sky over Edgartown Harbor.

"Wow!" said Barnaby. "We are actually flying!"

"Look at all the sailboats!" said Baxter.

"And there's the Lighthouse!" said Barnaby.

"It sure does look tiny from up here," said Baxter.

"Hold on tight, Baxter," said Barnaby, "unless you feel like taking a swim!"

As the wind grew stronger, they flew faster and higher.

"What are you two doing up there?" shouted a shopkeeper on North Water Street.

Barnaby and Baxter waved, but they were going too fast to stop and talk.

The kite took Barnaby and Baxter over Main Street past the Old Whaling Church.
The bell from the clock tower struck noon.

"I wish we had time to eat lunch," said Baxter. "I'm hungry!"

But the kite just kept flying.

"Now where are we going?" asked Barnaby.

"This kite sure does have a mind of its own," said Baxter.

Barnaby and Baxter held on tightly. They flew past the gazebo as they headed toward the little town of Oak Bluffs.

"Oh, look!" shouted Barnaby. "It's the Flying Horses Carousel."

"I love the Flying Horses!" said Baxter.

They were so excited that they let go of the kite string! Down, down they fell, but what luck! They landed right on a horse's back.

The Flying Horse took them around and around. Just as Barnaby reached for the brass ring, the Flying Horse came to life and jumped off the Carousel.

"Let's get out of here," said Freddie, the Flying Horse. "I haven't taken any time off in over a hundred years. I'll take you wherever you want to go."

"We just lost our kite," said Barnaby. "Will you help us find it?"

So Barnaby, Baxter, and Freddie flew high over West Tisbury.

"Hey! There goes our kite," said Barnaby.

"It's flying straight toward Takemmy Farm," said Freddie.

"Follow that kite!" cried Baxter.

When Barnaby, Baxter, and Freddie arrived at the Farm, all the animals greeted them.

"How d-d-do you d-d-do?" asked the giant Llama.

"It's a pleasure to meet you," said the Sheep.

"Are you new in town?" asked the Duck.

Freddie explained. "They are just visiting. They're trying to catch their kite."

"Have you seen it?" asked Baxter.

"It almost hit me in the head!" said the Rooster. "If I could fly, I would have caught it."

"Look! It's heading toward Vineyard Haven Harbor," cried Freddie.

"Let's hurry!" said Barnaby.

FRIENDLY
FARM
ANIMALS

"BON VOYAGE"

But when they arrived at the harbor docks, they saw that the kite had already flown out to sea.

"I would like to stay and help you," said Freddie, "but I have to get back to the Carousel."

Barnaby and Baxter hopped on board the nearest sailboat to try to catch their kite.

"Goodbye!" shouted Barnaby and Baxter to all their friends.

Just as Barnaby and Baxter were about to catch the kite, a huge wave from the schooner *Shenandoah* swept over them and flipped their boat.

Luckily, the fishing boat *Turtle II* happened to be nearby, and came to their rescue.

The *Turtle II* headed toward the fishing village of Menemsha. There, the fishermen checked their lobster pots. And Barnaby tried to catch a fish.

"I think I've caught a fish!" shouted Barnaby.

"Barnaby," said Baxter. "We are trying to catch a kite, not a fish."

Just as Barnaby was about to reel in the fish, the kite swooped right over his head.

"There it is!" shouted Baxter.

"Quick! Quick! Grab it," said Barnaby.

They jumped up and tried to catch the kite string…

THERE
GOES
THE KITE

but they missed and landed in the water once again!

A QUICK
SWIM

A WHALE
TO THE
RESCUE

Fortunately, Barnaby's good friend Hector the Whale saw them. "Hop on my back," he shouted.

"We have been trying to catch our kite all day long," explained Barnaby. "It's going to get dark soon. We don't have much time."

"I have an idea," said Hector.

Hector told Barnaby and Baxter about his plan. "When we get close to your kite, I will blow water from my spout. It will send you into the air. Then you can grab the kite string, and you'll be on your way."

"Ready?" asked Hector.

"I'm as ready as I'll ever be," said Barnaby. "Me too!" said Baxter.

"One…two…*three!*" shouted Hector. And up into the air Barnaby and Baxter flew.

Barnaby and Baxter caught the kite string!

"PHEW!" said Barnaby. "We got it!"

They held on tightly as the kite pulled them back…
back into the snowy winter night…

BACK INTO
WINTER

through the open window, and into their bedroom.

Tired from their busy day, Barnaby and Baxter fell sound asleep.